**Dear Parents and Teachers,**

In an easy-reader format, **My Readers** introduce classic stories to children who are learning to read. Although favorite characters and time-tested tales are the basis for **My Readers**, the books tell completely new stories and are freshly and beautifully illustrated.

My Readers are available in three levels:

 Level One is for the emergent reader and features repetitive language and word clues in the illustrations.

 Level Two is for more advanced readers who still need support saying and understanding some words. Stories are longer with word clues in the illustrations.

 Level Three is for independent, fluent readers who enjoy working out occasional unfamiliar words. The stories are longer and divided into chapters.

Encourage children to select books based on interests, not reading levels. Read aloud with children, showing them how to use the illustrations for clues. With adult guidance and rereading, children will eventually read the desired book on their own.

Here are some ways you might want to use this book with children:

- Talk about the title and the cover illustrations. Encourage the child to use these to predict what the story is about.
- Discuss the interior illustrations and try to piece together a story based on the pictures. Does the child want to change or adjust his first prediction?
- After children reread a story, suggest they retell or act out a favorite part.

My Readers will not only help children become readers, they will serve as an introduction to some of the finest classic children's books available today.

—LAURA ROBB
Educator and Reading Consultant

To the cats who rescued me: Whiskers, Felix, and Zoe
—T. F.

To Nadia
—O. I. & A. I.

SQUARE
FISH

An Imprint of Macmillan Children's Publishing Group

HARRY CAT AND TUCKER MOUSE: HARRY TO THE RESCUE!
Text copyright © 2011 by Thea Feldman. Illustrations copyright © 2011 by Olga and Aleksey Ivanov.
All rights reserved. Distributed in Canada by H.B. Fenn and Company Ltd.
Printed in January 2011 in China by Toppan Leefung Printing Ltd.,
Dongguan City, Guangdong Province.
For information, address Square Fish, 175 Fifth Avenue, New York, NY 10010.

Library of Congress Cataloging-in-Publication Data Available

ISBN: 978-0-312-62507-8 (hardcover)
1 3 5 7 9 10 8 6 4 2

ISBN: 978-0-312-62509-2 (paperback)
1 3 5 7 9 10 8 6 4 2

Book design by Patrick Collins/Véronique Lefèvre Sweet

Square Fish logo designed by Filomena Tuosto

First Edition: 2011

www.squarefishbooks.com
www.mackids.com

This is a Level 2 book

LEXILE 490L

Harry Cat and Tucker Mouse
HARRY TO THE RESCUE!

Story by Thea Feldman

Illustrated by Olga and Aleksey Ivanov

Inspired by the characters from
The Cricket in Times Square
written by George Selden and illustrated by Garth Williams

SQUARE
FISH

Macmillan Children's Publishing Group
New York

The Times Square
subway station was busy.
Tucker Mouse watched
from his home in the drainpipe.

He watched busy people hurrying by.

Tucker watched and waited.

Tucker waited for people

to drop things.

A button from a coat.

Sprinkles from an ice cream cone.

A wrapper from a stick of gum.

Tucker collected all these things—

and more!

Tucker loved his collection.

Most of all, he loved coins.

Pennies. Nickels. Dimes. Quarters.

Tucker had a stack of coins

in his drainpipe.

It was a tidy little life savings

for a mouse.

Plink!

Tucker knew that sound.

It was a coin hitting the floor.

A man in the shoeshine store

had dropped a penny.

The penny swirled and rolled,

and rolled and swirled,

before it landed

behind the shoeshine booth.

The man could not reach the penny.

It was in a space that was too small

for a human hand.

But Tucker knew the space was

just the right size for him.

Tucker waited until the station

and the store got less busy.

Then he ran across the way,

slipped behind the shoeshine booth,

and grabbed the shiny penny.

Suddenly, it was very dark.

The shoeshine store had closed!

Tucker looked for a way out.

There was just a thin crack

under the door.

There were no holes in the walls.

There were no holes in the ceiling.

Tucker was trapped!

Tucker waited for his friend
Harry Cat to come home.
When he saw Harry,
Tucker shouted,
"Help me, Harry!"

Harry was surprised to see Tucker

across the way in the store.

"Tucker, why are you

in the shoeshine store?" asked Harry.

"It's closed."

"I know that!" shouted Tucker.

He held up the penny.

"Ah," said Harry. "I understand."

Harry jumped up to see

if he could open the door,

but the door was locked tight.

Harry saw a sign on the door.

The sign read:

We're on vacation!

Closed for two weeks.

In case of emergency,

go to the Bellinis' newsstand.

Harry came up with a plan.

"Tucker?" asked Harry.

"Yes, Harry?" said Tucker.

"Do you see any food in there?"
asked Harry.

"Not a crumb," said Tucker,

"and I am getting hungry."

"I'll be back in a minute," said Harry.
Harry found thin pieces of a sandwich
and slid them under the door.

Once Tucker's belly was full,

Harry told him what the sign said.

"TWO WEEKS?" shouted Tucker.

"I'll die of hunger!"

"No, you won't," said Harry.

"I can feed you every night

when the station gets quiet."

"But I'll die from boredom,"
cried Tucker.
"And I'll be lonely,"
he said softly.
"Don't worry, I am going
to get you out," said Harry
as he ran off to get help.

It felt like a very long time to Tucker,

but Harry was only gone

for a little while.

He came back with their friends,

Lulu Pigeon and Ned Squirrel.

Lulu tried, but she couldn't pick the lock
with her beak.

"Ooo ooo ooo," said Lulu.

"That's quite a mousetrap."

Harry, Ned, and Lulu PUSHED

against the door.

It didn't budge.

"We'll have to think of something else,"

said Harry.

It was late.

Everyone was too tired to think.

Tucker looked at Harry in the drainpipe.

Harry looked at Tucker in the store.

"Don't worry," said Harry.

"I am going to get you out."

The next day, Harry still didn't know

what to do.

He watched as Mr. Smedley

stopped by the Bellinis' newsstand.

Every Sunday, Mr. Smedley

leaned over the counter

to tell Papa Bellini about

the latest opera he had seen.

Mr. Smedley and Papa Bellini

loved opera.

They loved it the way

Tucker loved coins.

Harry noticed that

one of Mr. Smedley's shoes was untied.

He thought about this.

Without a shoelace,

Mr. Smedley might trip.

Would a missing shoelace

be an "emergency"?

Would it get Papa Bellini

to open the shoeshine store?

Harry decided to see.

On quiet cat paws, Harry crept up

to the newsstand.

With one curved claw,

Harry tugged gently.

He looked up.

Mr. Smedley hadn't noticed a thing.

Harry gave another little tug.

And another. And another.

Harry kept tugging

until the shoelace was free!

Harry grabbed the shoelace

and raced back to the drainpipe.

As Mr. Smedley said good-bye

to Papa Bellini,

he turned and . . .

walked right out of his shoe!

Papa Bellini and Mr. Smedley

scratched their heads.

"Don't worry," said Papa Bellini.

"I have the key to the shoeshine store.

You can pay me for a new pair

of shoelaces."

Papa opened the shoeshine store
to get Mr. Smedley a new pair
of shoelaces.

No one but Harry

saw a little mouse with a penny

scurry in a hurry across the station.

No one but Harry

got the biggest hug

a little mouse could possibly give.

"You got me out!" shouted Tucker.

"I told you I would!" said Harry.

Mr. Smedley and Papa Bellini
never knew what happened
to Mr. Smedley's shoelace.
They never knew
that it became part of a collection
in a drainpipe.

And Mr. Smedley never knew
how a penny got into his shoe
the next time he visited
the Bellinis' newsstand.
He never knew
that it was one little mouse's big
"Thank You."

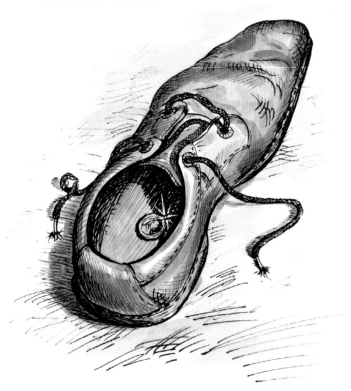